E. Bowe

© Aladdin Books Ltd 2001

Designed and produced by
Aladdin Books Ltd
28 Percy Street
London W1P 0LD

First published in
Great Britain in 2001 by
Franklin Watts
96 Leonard Street
London EC2A 4XD

ISBN 0 7496 4161 4
A catalogue record for this
book is available from the
British Library.

Printed in Belgium

All rights reserved

Editor
Bibby Whittaker

Literacy Consultant
Rosemary Chamberlin,
Westminster Institute of Education,
Oxford Brookes University

Design
Flick, Book Design and Graphics

Picture Research
Brian Hunter Smart

# READING ABOUT
# My Pet

By Jim Pipe

Aladdin/Watts
London • Sydney

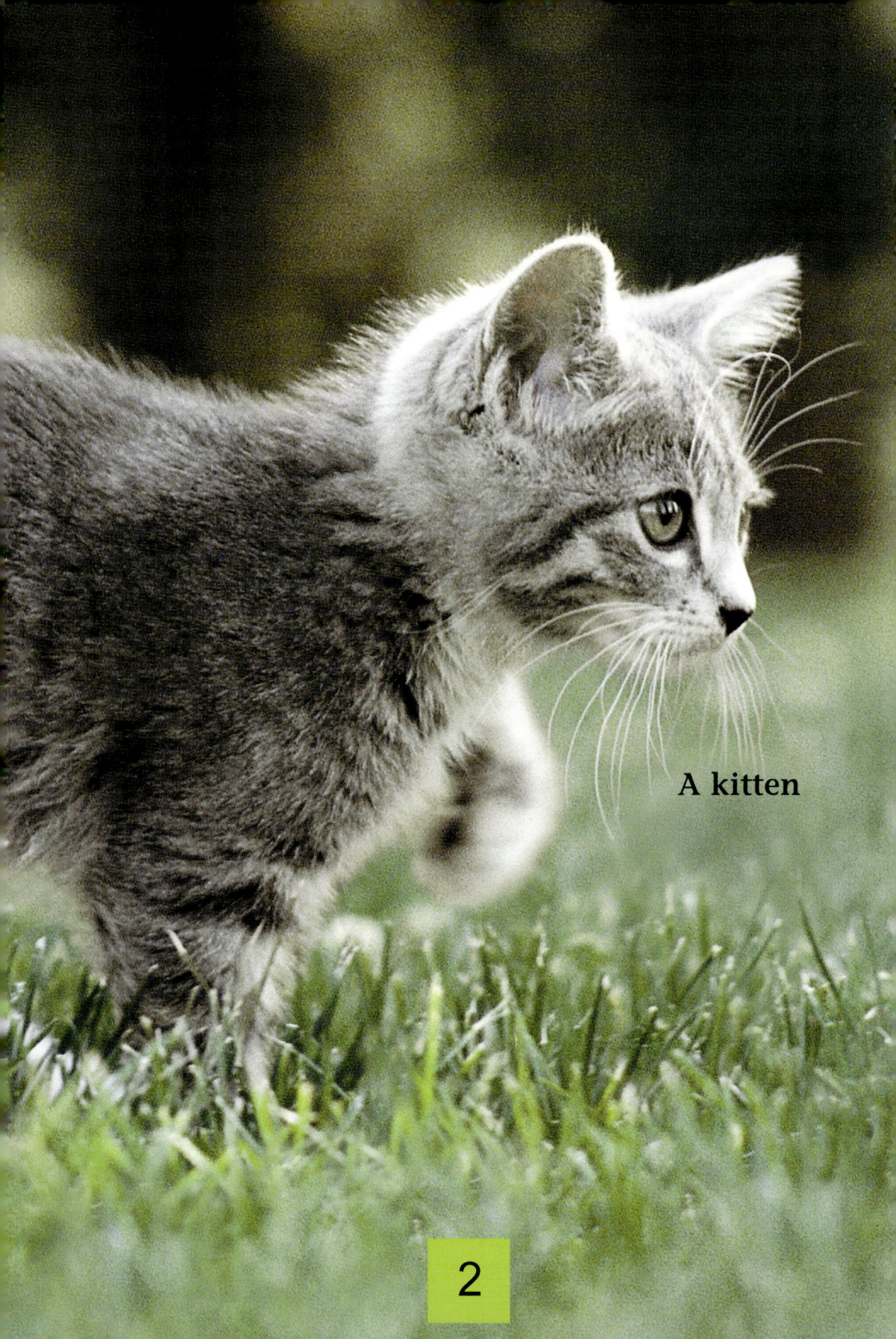

A kitten

My friend Pete has a kitten.

It likes to run across the room and grab some string.

"Look at my kitten," says Pete.

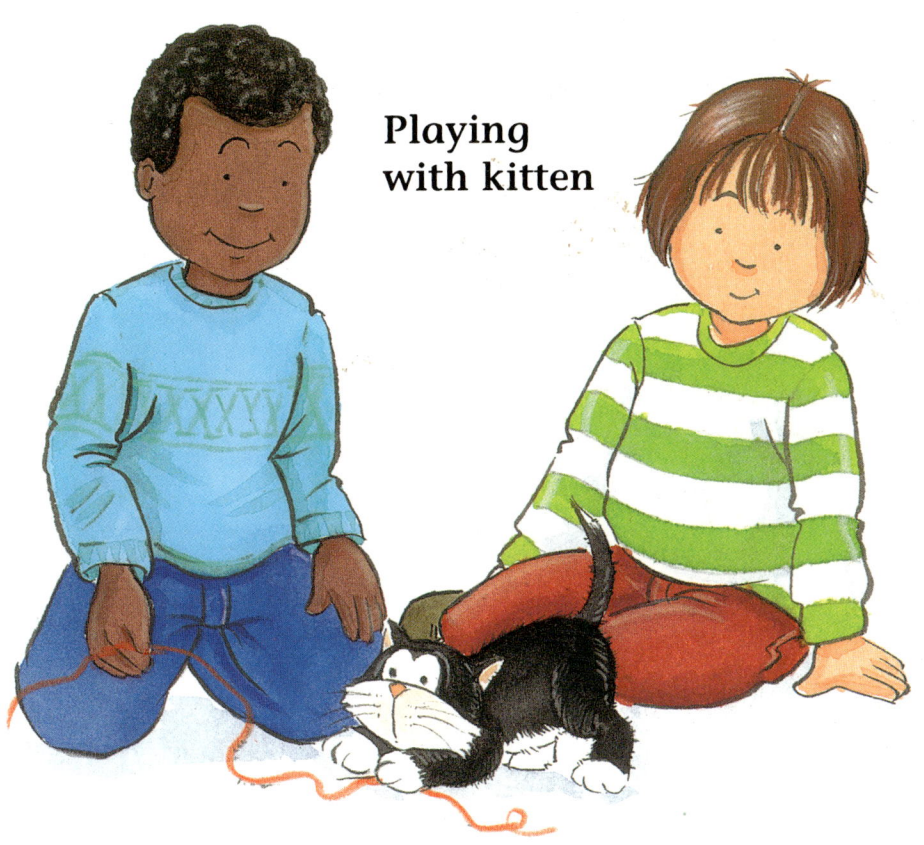

Playing with kitten

"Can I have a pet?" I ask Mum. "Please. I would love a puppy."

"Okay," says Mum. "But you must look after it. A puppy isn't a toy."

**Puppies**

So we go to get a puppy. There are lots of puppies to choose from.

Then I see the right one.

"I want that one," I say.

Choosing a puppy

We bring my new puppy home. She runs up and licks my hand.

"Look at her," I say. "I can't wait to show Pete."

"A puppy needs to sleep, too," says Mum.

A puppy's bed

We get a box and a blanket,
to make a bed for my puppy.

My puppy cries and cries.

"Look at her," I say.
"Does she feel sick?"

"No," says Dad.
"Puppy is hungry."

Feeding puppy

Dad and I get food and water. We feed my puppy at the same time each day.

Puppy eats a lot. Just like me!

A puppy eating

My puppy likes to chew on shoes.

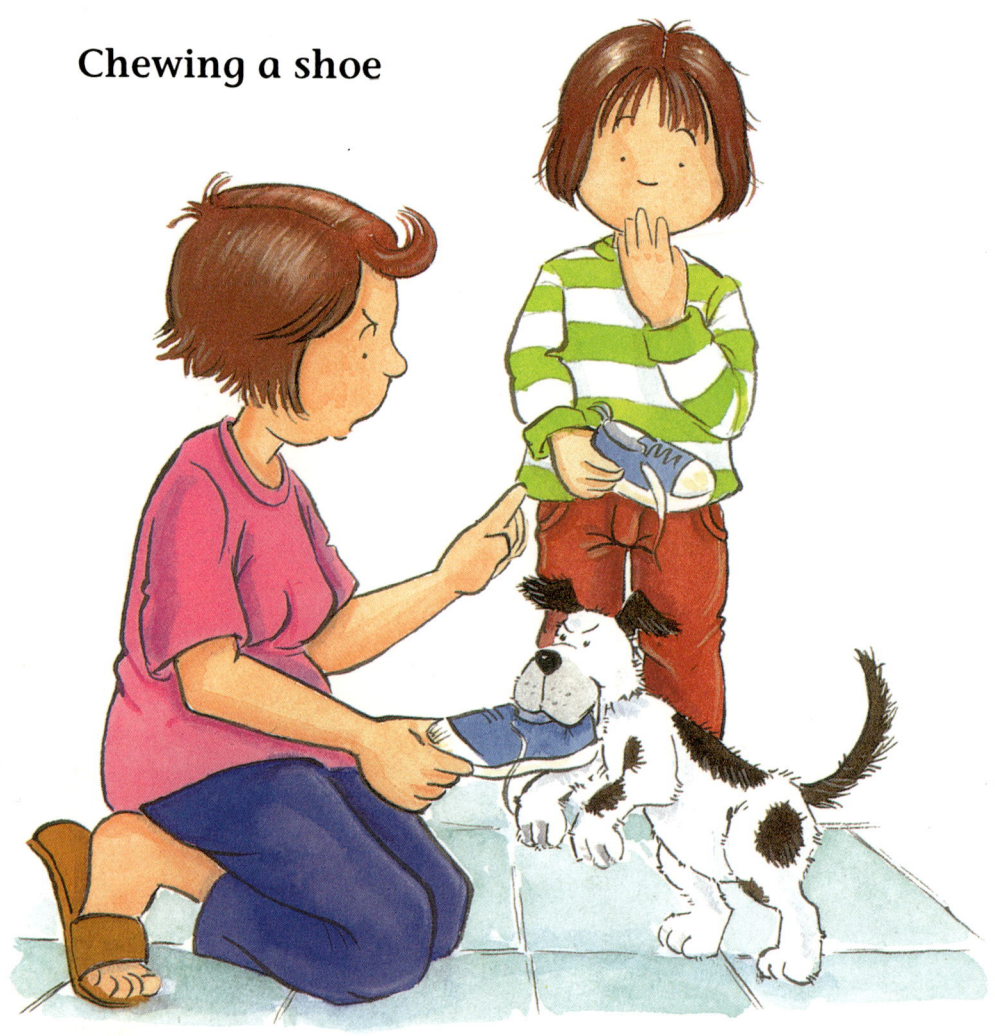

Chewing a shoe

"Look at her," I say.

"Is she still hungry?"

Dad says puppies like to chew when their teeth are growing.

"But puppy must *not* chew on our good shoes," says Mum.

Bone

So we buy puppy a bone to chew.

My puppy leaves a puddle on the floor.

"Oh, look," I say. "What a mess!"

Mum says, "We must teach puppy to go outside".

Puddle

Puppy outside

Puppies are smart.

They learn to go outside.

My puppy learns to wait for me.

Then I take her out.

Mum says, "A puppy likes to run and play, just like you".

So we take puppy to the park to run and play. Pete comes too.

"We must teach puppy to walk on a lead," Pete says.

At first puppy pulls hard. But soon she learns to walk with us.

On a lead

A dog shakes its coat

At the park, my puppy jumps into a puddle of water.

She gives herself a shake and water flies all over.

"Look at her," says Pete. "What a mess she is!"

So we take puppy home. Pete dries her and I brush her coat.

Drying puppy

One day, my puppy looks sad.
She does not want to play or eat.

"Look at her, Mum," I say.
"Is she sick?"

A sick puppy

"Don't worry," says Mum.

"We can take her to a doctor."

The animal doctor is called a vet.
She helps sick pets get better.

At the vet's

I worry about my puppy. Now I know that she is not just for fun.

"Give puppy this medicine," says the vet, "and she will feel better".

Soon my puppy is well. She wags her tail and wants to play.

"Look at her," I say to Pete. "My puppy is so much better."

A happy puppy

Here are some words and phrases from the book.

Play with a kitten

Feed the puppy

Puddle

Lots of puppies

On a lead

Dry the coat

Chew a shoe

Choose a puppy

Can you use these words to write your own story?

# Did you see these in the book?

Paw

Ear

Whiskers

Collar

**Illustrator:** Mary Lonsdale for SGA

**Picture Credits:**
*Abbreviations: t – top, m – middle, b – bottom, r – right, l – left, c – centre.* 2, 24mr – Digital Stock. 4, 22 – Tim Wright/CORBIS. 7, 13, 16, 18, 24tl, 24tr, 24ml – Corbis; 9, 11, 15, 21, 23, – Select Pictures.